Karen's School Picture

**Here are some other books
about Karen
that you might enjoy:**

Little Sister

Karen's School Picture
Ann M. Martin

Illustrations by Susan Tang

A
LITTLE APPLE
PAPERBACK

SCHOLASTIC INC.
New York Toronto London Auckland Sydney

No part of this publication may be reproduced in whole or in part, or stored in a retrieval system, or transmitted in any form or by any means, electronic, mechanical, photocopying, recording, or otherwise, without written permission of the publisher. For information regarding permission, write to Scholastic Inc., 730 Broadway, New York, NY 10003.

ISBN 0-590-42672-9

Copyright © 1989 by Ann M. Martin. All rights reserved. Published by Scholastic Inc. APPLE PAPERBACKS is a registered trademark of Scholastic Inc. BABY-SITTERS LITTLE SISTER is a trademark of Scholastic Inc.

12 11 10 9 8 7 6 5 4 3 2 1   9/8 0 1 2 3 4/9

Printed in the U.S.A.   11

First Scholastic printing, September 1989

*This book is for
Ashley Vinsel*

School Pictures

"Hi, Ms. Colman! Hi, Ms. Colman!" I cried.

Ms. Colman is my second-grade teacher. She is very, very, very nice. She always helps kids and never yells at them. So I like her a lot.

Some kids don't like school, but I do. I like school on Monday mornings. I even like school when it gives me a headache or makes my eyes hurt. School can do that to you, you know.

I am Karen Brewer. I am six years old. I

am only supposed to be in first grade, but after I started first grade, my teacher said, "Karen can do second-grade work. Let's put her in second grade." So Mommy and Daddy said okay, and the next thing I knew, I was in Ms. Colman's class.

That was fine with me. My two best friends are Hannie Papadakis and Nancy Dawes. They were already in Ms. Colman's class. They sat in the back row. Ms. Colman said I could sit next to them if the three of us promised to pay attention. We are pretty good about paying attention, but sometimes I have to let Nancy smell my strawberry eraser or something. Then Ms. Colman just says, "Back to work, girls."

There are sixteen kids in my class. We sit at desks in rows — four rows of four desks. The fourth person in my row is Ricky Torres. He is a pest. Luckily he sits at one end of the row and I sit at the other end. Hannie is the one who got stuck sitting next to him.

"Good morning, Karen," my teacher replied.

It was a Monday morning and I bounced into our classroom. Another week of school was about to begin. Another week of worksheets and gym and stories.

Ms. Colman smiled at me and I smiled back.

I ran to my desk and checked on my strawberry eraser. There it was. Then I hung my coat on my hook in the coat room. When I came out I saw Hannie and Nancy.

"Hi! Hi, you guys!" I cried.

Nancy lives next door to me and sometimes we ride to school together, but not that morning.

"Look what I got," said Hannie. She held out a purse shaped like a cat. Hannie and I like cats a lot.

"Aw, how adorable. How cuuuuuute," said a voice.

Hannie and Nancy and I looked up. It was Ricky Torres.

"Be quiet, Yicky Ricky," I said.

Ricky opened his mouth to say something mean back to me. Before he could, Ms.

Colman clapped her hands. "Time to get ready for attendance," she announced.

Another day of school had begun.

Guess what. It turned out not to be just *any* old day. At the very end, Ms. Colman said, "Class, I have a special announcement. In two weeks, it will be school-picture day. Each of you will have your own picture taken, and then we will have our class picture taken. All of us together."

4

"Oh, goody!" I couldn't help exclaiming.

I just *love* having my picture taken. I love to get dressed up. I love to tie a ribbon in my hair. School-picture day would be very wonderful.

I was so excited that I ignored Yicky Ricky when he said in a high, silly voice, "Oh, goody!" just like I had done.

I didn't even pay attention to the headache I had. Or to my eyes, which were hurting again. All I could think about was what I would wear the day our pictures were taken.

"Let's stand together in the class picture," I whispered to Nancy.

"Yeah!" she replied. She passed the message on to Hannie.

Hannie grinned at me.

What a great day it had been! How could I wait two whole weeks to have my picture taken?

Two Families

"Mommy! Hey, Mommy! In two weeks it will be school-picture day!" I called.

Nancy and I ran out of Stoneybrook Academy. That is the private school we go to. Hannie's brother Linny goes there, too, and someday her baby sister Sari and my little brother Andrew will go there. Nancy doesn't have any brothers or sisters.

"School-picture day," said Mommy. "I can tell you are very excited."

"Yes," I said, as Nancy and I climbed in the car. "I can't wait to get all those little pictures. The ones you can cut up and give to special people after you write, 'Love, Karen' on the backs."

"Am I a special person?" spoke up Andrew, who was sitting in the front seat next to Mommy. Andrew is four.

"Of course you are," I replied. Then I added grandly, "You can have two pictures if there are enough."

I settled back against the seat while Mommy

drove Nancy and Andrew and me home. My head hurt. I rubbed my eyes.

I saw Mommy glancing at me in the rearview mirror.

"I have a headache," I told her. "Another one."

"We worked very hard in school today," Nancy told my mother.

"And you are a busy girl, Karen," added Mommy. "You have homework now, and meetings of the Fun Club."

I nodded. My headaches always went away after I'd been home for awhile.

"Karen?" said Andrew, turning around to look at me. "Are you going to give pictures to everyone in the little house and everyone in the big house?"

"Yup," I replied.

The people in the little house are Mommy and Andrew and Seth and me. Seth is my stepfather. His last name is Engle, so Mommy's last name is Engle now, too. But Andrew and I are still Brewers, like Daddy. Also at the little house are Midgie and

Rocky, but they are a dog and a cat. I will not need to give them pictures.

The people at the big house are Daddy and Elizabeth and Charlie and Sam and Kristy and David Michael and Emily Michelle and Nannie. And Andrew and me when we visit them. Oh, and Shannon and Boo-Boo. They are another dog and cat. They won't need pictures, either. Even so, I wonder if I will have enough pictures for my friends *and* for everyone in my two families.

That's what the big house and the little house are. The places where my two families live. A long time ago, Mommy and Daddy got divorced. Then they each got married again. Elizabeth is Daddy's wife. She's my stepmother. And Charlie, Sam, Kristy, and David Michael are Elizabeth's kids. They're my stepbrothers and stepsister. Emily Michelle is my adopted sister. Daddy and Elizabeth adopted her. She came all the way from a country called Vietnam. She is only two years old. And Nannie is Elizabeth's mother, so she is sort of my grandmother.

I call myself Karen Two-Two. I call my brother Andrew Two-Two. That's because once Ms. Colman read our class a book called *Jacob Two-Two Meets the Hooded Fang*. I think the name Karen Two-Two is just right for me since I have two of everything. I have two houses. I have two families (one at each house). I have two dogs (one at each house) and two cats (one at each house). In fact, I have lots of twos that are one at each house — a stuffed cat named Goosie at the little house and a stuffed cat named Moosie at the big house, clothes at the little house and clothes at the big house, toys at the little house and toys at the big house. Andrew does, too. We live at the big house every other weekend, so when we go there, we don't have to remember to take a lot of things with us.

It might sound like fun being a two-two, and usually it is. But sometimes it isn't. For instance, I only had one special blanket, Tickly, and I had to rip Tickly in half so that

10

I could have a piece at the big house and a piece at the little house. I didn't mind too much, though. I just said, "Ouch," for Tickly and then it was over.

As we drove home from school that day, I closed my eyes to make them stop hurting.

I practiced a movie-star smile. I forgot about my eyes and about being a two-two, and thought of school pictures instead.

Karen's Turn to Read

Friday, Friday, Friday! Every other Friday, Andrew and I get ready to leave the little house and stay with Daddy and our big-house family for the weekend.

Mommy drives us over. Andrew and I are always very excited. I was so excited that my aching eyes didn't bother me. We don't usually do anything very special at the big house. I just like being with my other family.

Maybe I better tell you about the people in my other family, since there are so many of them. The big house sounds confusing, but it isn't.

First there are Daddy and Elizabeth. They are the parents. They are also stepparents to each other's kids. Elizabeth is a very nice stepmother to Andrew and me. And I think that Daddy is a nice stepfather to Kristy and her brothers.

Charlie and Sam are Elizabeth's two oldest kids. They are so old they are in high school.

Then there is Kristy. She is thirteen. She is one of my favorite, favorite people in the big house or anywhere. Kristy does a lot of baby-sitting. She even has a business called the Baby-sitters Club. Sometimes she sits for Andrew and David Michael and Emily and me.

David Michael is my eight-year-old stepbrother. Mostly he is a pain like Ricky Torres. But at least he collects bugs, so that's okay.

Emily Michelle is the youngest person at the big house. Before Daddy and Elizabeth adopted her, Andrew was the youngest person. And I was the youngest girl. Sometimes I am not sure how I feel about Emily. She's too little to play with — but she's awfully cute. I feel like I don't know her very well, though.

After Emily moved in, so did Nannie. Nannie is Kristy's favorite grandmother. She takes care of Emily when Daddy and Elizabeth are at work and everyone else is at school.

And then, of course, there are Shannon and Boo-Boo. The big house is very full and busy. When Andrew and I are visiting, ten people and two pets live there. That is one reason I like the big house so much. There is always something going on.

Most nights, I do not like to go to bed. I would rather stay up. I do not want to miss out on anything. But when Daddy says, "Bedtime, Karen," he means bedtime.

Kristy always makes bedtime easier. When my nightgown is on and I am under the covers with Moosie and Tickly, Kristy comes into my room. She always says, "What book shall we read tonight?"

For the longest time, I would answer, "*The Witch Next Door*," since I think Mrs. Porter, our next-door neighbor, is a witch. Now Kristy and I read chapter books. We had finished *Charlotte's Web*. So I said, "How about starting *Mrs. Piggle-Wiggle*?"

"Fine," replied Kristy. She found the book on my shelf. She brought it to my bed. Then she climbed onto my bed and sat next to

me. "Do you want to read first?" she asked. (Kristy and I take turns reading.)

"Okay," I said.

I read the first page.

I read the second page.

I was supposed to read four more pages, until I got to the middle of the first chapter. Then Kristy would finish the chapter. But my eyes were hurting again.

"Kristy," I said, after page two, "I can't read anymore. My eyes hurt. So does my head."

"You must be tired," said Kristy. "You've had a long week. I'll finish the chapter for you. Maybe," she added, "you should slow down a little. You do an awful lot for someone who is six."

"Almost seven," I reminded her.

"Even so."

Kristy did finish the chapter. It was very funny. By the time she was done, my headache was gone.

Karen's Headache

Blechhh.

I like Saturdays. I like *any* Saturday. But a sunny Saturday is better than a rainy Saturday. And when I woke up the next morning, I found a rainy Saturday. I found a dreary, gray, wet, blechhh day.

But do you know what Daddy said that morning after breakfast? He said, "Today is a perfect day."

"Perfect for what?" replied Sam. "Ducks?"

I giggled.

"No," said Daddy. "Perfect for building

a fire in the fireplace and reading aloud. That would be very cozy."

Usually Sam and Charlie go off on the weekends. They do grown-up things with their high-school friends. But that day they didn't have any plans. They did not seem very excited about reading aloud by the fire, but they couldn't think of anything else to do.

So in a little while, my whole big-house family was sitting in the living room. Daddy had made a roaring fire. It was crackling and popping. It shot orange sparks up the chimney.

Shannon and Boo-Boo lay down on the rug in front of the fireplace. Daddy and Elizabeth sat on the couch. Elizabeth held Emily in her lap. I sat in Kristy's lap in an armchair. Nannie sat in another armchair. And all the boys — Andrew, David Michael, Sam, and Charlie — sat around on the floor.

"What are we going to read?" I asked.

"We are going to start a book called *Mrs.*

Frisby and the Rats of NIMH," replied Daddy.

"I know that story!" cried Andrew.

"Yes," said Daddy, "but you have only seen it on a video cassette. The story in the book is a little different."

"It's longer," said David Michael.

"But I think you will like it," spoke up Elizabeth. "It's a story that both grown-ups and children can enjoy."

"We'll take turns reading," said Daddy. "I'll start. Then anyone who wants to can take a turn."

So Daddy put on his reading glasses. He began the story about Mrs. Frisby, the mother mouse, who has to move her children and her house before the farmer with the big plow comes and runs over them. Elizabeth was right. Even Sam and Charlie were interested in the story. It was not a baby book.

After Daddy read for awhile, Elizabeth took a turn. Then Charlie, and then Kristy. When Kristy was finished, she said, "Karen do you want a turn? Some of these words are hard, but you're a very good reader."

"Okay," I said. But after about half a page, my head hurt again.

"This story is too hard," I said. "I give up my turn."

"Karen, you were doing just fine," Kristy told me. "I know the print is small, but you read every word perfectly." She paused. After a moment she said, "Hey, last night you got a headache reading *Mrs. Piggle-Wiggle* and gave up your turn then, too. What's going on?"

"Try reading again," Daddy suggested to me. "Hold the book closer."

I tried. The words swam before my eyes. I held the book farther away. That wasn't any better.

"Hmm," said Daddy. "It seems to me that your work in school has not been as good as usual lately. I think maybe you need to see an ophthalmologist."

"A what?" I asked.

"An eye doctor."

"An eye doctor! You mean to get *glasses?* No way. I don't want glasses!"

"Well, you may need them. After all, your mom wears glasses. And I wear glasses for reading. It makes sense."

I didn't say another word. But I was *not* going to get glasses.

Rocky's Tail

Usually, when Mommy picks Andrew and me up at Daddy's on Sunday night, she just pulls the car into the drive and honks. Then Andrew and I say good-bye to everyone at the big house and run out to the car.

But tonight, Daddy walked out to the car with us. "Listen," he said to Mommy, "I need to talk to you. I think Karen needs to see an eye doctor. She's been getting lots of headaches."

"That's true," said Mommy.

"And her schoolwork hasn't been as good as usual lately."

"I know."

"And this weekend, we realized that every time Karen has to read something, especially if the print is small, she gets a headache. Or she squints her eyes. Or she holds the book closer or farther away."

"I'll make an appointment with Doctor Gourson tomorrow," said Mommy.

"Nooooo!" I howled.

"She doesn't want glasses," Daddy said to Mommy. He whispered, but I heard him anyway.

"Of course I don't!" I exclaimed. "They'll make me look funny."

"But think how much better you'll feel," said Mommy.

"No glasses," I said flatly, as we drove away.

"We'll see," replied Mommy.

The next day, Mrs. Dawes, Nancy's

mother, drove Nancy and me home from school. As usual, my head ached and my eyes hurt. But when I walked into our kitchen, I said, "Hi, Mommy! Guess what. My head doesn't hurt at all. My eyes do not hurt, either. I think I just had a virus. Maybe I had the flu or a very bad head cold."

Mommy smiled at me. "I'm glad you're feeling better," she said.

"I think I will fix a snack," I said. "Maybe Andrew would like one, too. Andrew!" I called.

"What?" he answered. He ran into the kitchen.

"Would you like a snack?" I asked him. "I will fix us Oreo cookies and milk."

"Sure!" said Andrew.

I am always starving when I get home from school. I need food right away. "You get the cookies, I'll get the milk and the glasses," I told Andrew.

Andrew put the package of cookies on

the kitchen table. I set out two glasses. Then I carried the big carton of milk to the table. I opened it and began to pour.

SPLOOSH!

"Karen! Look at what you're doing!" cried Mommy, jumping up.

I looked. I was pouring milk . . . wasn't I?

"Karen, stop!" exclaimed Andrew.

I stopped. I looked at the table. I leaned over and looked more closely. I had poured

the milk, but I had missed the glass. The milk was all over the table. It was running onto the floor.

I couldn't help it. I began to cry.

"I'm sorry!" I said. I ran out of the kitchen.

"Look out, Karen!" I heard Andrew shout from behind me.

Too late. I tripped over Rocky and stepped on his tail. I hadn't even seen him.

"MROW!" cried Rocky angrily. He turned around and began licking his tail.

I couldn't blame him for being mad. I flopped on the couch in the living room and cried and cried. Soon I felt someone sit down next to me. Then Mommy's voice said, "Don't worry, honey. I called Doctor Gourson today. I made an appointment for you to see him on Thursday."

I nodded miserably. I didn't want glasses. Not at all. But I felt terrible about Rocky. And besides, my head really did hurt. So did my eyes.

The Ophthalmologist

The only good thing about going to Dr. Gourson was that my appointment was at twelve-thirty in the afternoon. I got to miss over two hours of school. Even though I like school, a little vacation is always nice. I felt very important when Ms. Colman looked at her watch and said it was time to go meet Mommy. Everyone else was stuck working on subtraction problems. I got to put on my jacket and leave. I knew my classmates were watching me and wishing they could leave, too.

Mommy and I had to sit for a very long time in the waiting room at Dr. Gourson's office. I never understand that. How come doctors always tell you to come so early? It is a gigundo waste of time.

"Mommy, I'm bored," I said. I wished Andrew were there, but he was staying with Mrs. Dawes while we were at Dr. Gourson's.

Mommy gave me a pad of paper and a pencil. "Why don't you draw some pictures?" she suggested.

I drew a picture of everyone in my two families. Then I put glasses on each person. Except me.

A nurse came to the doorway of the waiting room. "Karen Brewer?" he said.

Mommy and I stood up. We followed the nurse into a dim room. Lots and lots of machines and equipment were in it.

"Have a seat right here," said the nurse. Then he left.

I climbed into a big chair. It was like a dentist's chair.

Mommy sat on a regular chair nearby.

Dr. Gourson made us wait a while longer. At last he came in.

"Hi," he said. "I'm Doctor Gourson. You must be Karen."

I nodded.

Mommy and Dr. Gourson already knew each other. They said hello. Then they talked about me and my eyes. Finally, Dr. Gourson pointed to a chart on the wall across the room. At the top of the chart were some big E's. They looked like this:

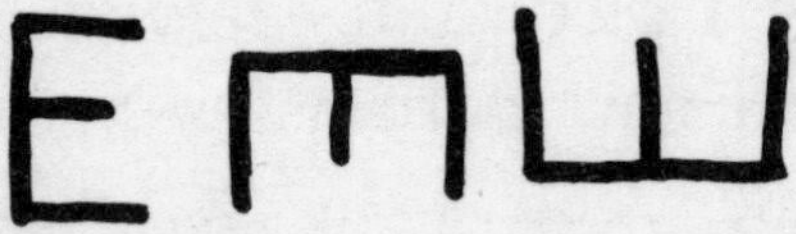

"Show me which way the E's are pointing," said the doctor.

So I did. That was easy. See? I didn't need glasses after all.

Next Dr. Gourson said, "Karen, how old are you?"

"Six," I replied.

"And do you know the letters in the alphabet?" he asked.

"Of course I do. Mommy told you I can read," I said to him. What a silly question.

"Karen," said Mommy warningly.

"Sorry," I told the doctor.

"That's quite all right," he replied. "Then start with the top row of letters and read down as far as you can."

I began reading. I read one row. Two rows. By the third row, the letters were a big blur.

"I can't read anymore," I had to tell Dr. Gourson. "But it isn't because I *can't read*. It's just that I can't see those little letters from way back here."

"Okay," replied the doctor. Then he did a whole lot of other things with my eyes.

First he put drops in them. The drops made my eyes run.

Then he looked at my eyes through all sorts of instruments. I didn't have to do anything but sit there, or, sometimes roll my eyes around, while he looked.

At last he said, "Karen? Mrs. Engle? You may go back to the waiting room now."

(The waiting room? Again?) "The nurse will call you in a little while and we can talk about Karen's eyes."

Oh, goody. Hurray. Just what I wanted.

The waiting room was even more boring this time than before. That was because those drops had made my eyes so blurry that I could hardly see. I couldn't read or draw pictures or do anything.

So Mommy read to me while we waited.

Karen's Glasses

"Karen Brewer?" said the nurse again.

Mommy and I stood up, and Mommy followed the nurse back to Dr. Gourson's office. She had to lead me by the hand. I could not see where I was going.

Dr. Gourson was sitting behind a desk in his office. Mommy and I sat on the other side of the desk. I sat in Mommy's lap.

"Well, Karen does need glasses," Dr. Gourson began. "She needs them pretty badly."

"Just for reading?" I asked hopefully. "Like Daddy and Seth?"

"No, I'm afraid not. You'll need them for reading and for all the time. In fact, you'll need two pairs of glasses."

"Two pairs!" I exclaimed. What would I do with two pairs of glasses?

"Yes," said the doctor. "You'll need one pair of glasses to help you see clearly when you're reading or doing other things up close. You'll need a second pair to help you see clearly the rest of the time."

I couldn't believe it. Glasses. I would never look like a movie star if I had to wear glasses. I almost began to cry, but I stopped myself.

Dr. Gourson gave Mommy a slip of paper. "These are the prescriptions for Karen's lenses," he told her. "There's an optometrist right here in the building, and — "

"What's an optometrist?" I interrupted.

"He's a person who makes glasses," said Dr. Gourson. "You can choose the frames you like. Then the optometrist will put the right lenses into them so that you'll be able to see."

Mommy and I left Dr. Gourson's office. We walked down a hallway. Mommy opened a door with some blurry letters on it. We went inside and she stepped up to a desk. A woman was standing behind the desk.

"Hello," Mommy said to the woman. "I am Mrs. Engle. This is my daughter, Karen. We have just come from Doctor Gourson's office. Karen needs two pairs of glasses." She handed the woman the slip of paper.

The woman looked at me and smiled. "Two pairs of glasses for Karen Engle," she said.

"Brewer," I corrected her. (That is another problem with being a two-two.)

Mommy explained about our names. Then the woman gave the prescription to the optometrist. When she came back, she said, "Let's look at frames. What kind of glasses do you want, Karen?"

"No glasses," I told her.

"Karen," said Mommy.

"Sorry," I said. "Um, I don't know what kind of glasses I want."

"Well, I'll show you some things. You will probably want different frames so that you can tell your reading glasses from your other glasses."

"Okay," I said.

"Come sit here," said the woman. She led me to a counter and lifted me onto a stool. My eyes were starting to clear up from the drops. I could see racks and racks of glasses frames on the counter. In front of me was a big mirror.

I tried on lots of glasses. I tried on white ones. I tried on round tan ones like Mommy's and square brown ones like Daddy's and gold-rimmed ones like Seth's.

"Yuck," I said about each pair.

Then the woman showed me a pair of pink glasses.

"Pink!" I exclaimed. "I can get *pink* glasses?!"

"They come in blue, too," said the woman. "A nice pale blue."

"I'll take them!" I said.

Mommy and the lady smiled.

When the optometrist had put the lenses in my glasses, Mommy and I walked out to the car. I put on my pink glasses. My blue glasses were going to be the ones for reading.

"I cannot believe it!" I cried. "Everything looks so much clearer. Brighter, too."

I knew I would never be a movie star now, but it was nice to see clearly again.

Glasses Everywhere!

Mommy and I got home just after school let out. I spent most of the afternoon trying on my two pairs of glasses and looking at myself in the mirror.

"I do not look so bad," I said to Goosie. Goosie was in the bathroom with me. I held him up to the mirror. "See? I do not look bad at all. I still look pretty much like Karen Brewer — wearing glasses."

Before I left school that day, Ms. Colman had given me my homework. I took it into the kitchen when Mommy began making dinner.

Mommy stood at the kitchen counter, reading a recipe. She was wearing her tan glasses.

I sat at the table with my workbook. I was wearing my blue glasses. (The words in the workbook were nice and clear.)

I thought of Seth and Daddy at work. They were probably wearing their glasses.

When Andrew came into the kitchen with his fire truck, I realized something.

"Hey, Andrew!" I exclaimed. "You're the only person at the little house who *doesn't* wear glasses. There are glasses everywhere!"

"So?" said Andrew. He sounded cross.

"Don't be mad," I told him. "It's okay if you don't need glasses. Hey, Mommy, this workbook page is really easy. I can read every single word."

"Good," said Mommy. "That sounds like my old Karen."

I finished my workbook pages in record

time. Mommy checked them. I had answered every question right!

I put my workbook away. Then I took off my blue glasses and put on my pink ones. I looked at myself in the bathroom mirror again. This time I tried out my movie-star smile. Even with glasses it looked okay.

"Mommy!" I called. "Can I go over to Nancy's and show her my glasses?"

"Yes," she replied. "But be home in half an hour. It's almost dinnertime."

"Okay!"

I ran out our front door, across our lawn, across Nancy's driveway, and along the walk to *her* front door. I was still wearing my pink glasses. I was carrying the blue ones in a case that the optometrist had given Mommy and me for free.

Ding-dong!

Nancy answered the door.

"Hi, Karen!" she cried. "Oh, you got them!"

I nodded. "Do you like them?"

"You know what? You don't look that different."

"I don't?"

"Nope."

That was good to know. "But do you like them?" I asked again.

"Sure," replied Nancy. "They're neat."

"Can I come in? I'll show you the other pair. I had to get *two* pairs."

Nancy let me inside. I modeled the blue glasses for her. Then I modeled both pairs of glasses for her mother. Then her father came home. I modeled them for him, too.

Mrs. Dawes said I looked lovely.

Mr. Dawes said I looked dashing.

I went home. I modeled my glasses for Seth. He said I looked grown up.

I was feeling a lot better about wearing glasses.

That night, I tried the pink glasses on Goosie. I tried the blue ones on my stuffed elephant. Then I took them off and put them on two of my dolls.

"Hey, Andrew!" I called. "Come here."

Andrew came into my room. He looked at the dolls. "See?" he said as I took the glasses off the dolls. "I am not the only one around here who does not wear glasses."

We laughed. "Rocky and Midgie don't wear them, either," I pointed out.

When Andrew left, I looked through the clothes in my closet. I decided that the next day I would wear my jeans and my unicorn shirt to school. The shirt is pink and blue with a white satin unicorn on the front. No matter which pair of glasses I wore, they would match my outfit. I would not look like a movie star, but I would look lovely and dashing and grown up.

I was ready for school.

Yicky Ricky

The next morning, I woke up with a funny feeling in my stomach.

"Mommy?" I said, when I went into the kitchen for breakfast. "I don't feel too good. My stomach feels jumpy."

"Does it hurt?" she asked. She put her hand on my forehead to see if I had a fever.

"No," I replied.

"Are you nervous about wearing your glasses to school today?"

"Yes."

Mommy smiled. "It won't be so bad. Your

friends have seen other kids in glasses."

"They haven't seen me," I told her.

But when I got to school, it *wasn't* too bad. Nancy and Hannie and I were the first ones to reach our classroom. Even Ms. Colman wasn't there.

Nancy had already seen my glasses, so she didn't say anything about them. But Hannie said, "Oh, cool! Pink glasses!"

"Do you really like them?" I asked.

"I really do."

The other kids started to arrive. Some of them didn't even notice my glasses. Two of them just said, "Oh, Karen, you got glasses."

Then Ms. Colman came in.

"Why, Karen," she said. "I like your glasses very much."

"So do I," said Natalie Springer. Natalie Springer is in my class, too. She is the only other person who wears glasses. Hers have gold rims. Natalie has worn glasses since before kindergarten.

"Thank you," I said to Ms. Colman and Natalie. Then I added, "Guess what. I have two pairs of glasses. I have blue ones for reading and these pink ones for the rest of the time."

"Gosh," said Natalie. She looked impressed.

But nobody else was paying much attention. Whew!

Then Ricky Torres came in. He saw me and my glasses right away.

"Ooh-ooh. Four-eyes!" he cried. "Hey, Karen. Are you just blind or are you as blind as an ugly old bat?"

"You are so dumb, Ricky," I said. "I am not blind at all. With my glasses on, I can see just fine. And besides, I think it's mean to tease about being blind. What if I really *were* blind?"

Ricky has hated me ever since the time I broke my wrist and he broke his ankle. We got casts at the same time. Each of us got lots of people to sign our casts. Ricky even got some baseball player to sign his. But *I* got a witch and an actress and Mr. Tastee to sign *my* cast. The witch was old Mrs.

Porter who lives next door to Daddy. The actress was a friend of Mommy's. And Mr. Tastee drives the Mr. Tastee ice-cream truck all over town. The kids in our class liked my autographs better than Ricky's.

Ricky has never forgiven me for that.

"Blind as a bat," Ricky said one more time, just to make me mad.

I looked at Ms. Colman. She was writing on the chalkboard. Her back was turned, so I stuck my tongue out at Ricky.

He did not stick his out at me, though. Instead he said, "School pictures are coming up, Miss Movie Star Brewer. Just think how *your* picture will look now."

I hadn't thought about that, but I didn't see what the big problem was.

"So I won't wear my glasses when the photographer takes my picture, Mr. Smarty-pants," I whispered loudly to Ricky. "You are so stupid. I can take my glasses off for a minute."

Ms. Colman clapped her hands. "Okay, class. Take your seats, please."

I stuck my tongue out at Ricky again. This time he stuck his out at me.

Then we sat down at our desks.

Teacher's Pet

All morning, Ricky called me Four-eyes and Bat-woman. He only whispered the names, so Ms. Colman wouldn't hear him.

All morning, I tried to ignore him.

That was not too hard.

First of all, we had art class. I just love art class. It is gigundo fun. Mr. Mackey comes into our room with his art cart, which is loaded with very wonderful supplies: paint and paper and crayons and glue and Magic Markers and scraps of things. Then he tells us what we are going to make.

"Today," he said, "we will make outer space pictures."

I wore my pink glasses while I listened to Mr. Mackey. I switched to my blue ones when I began my picture.

"Bat-woman!" whispered Ricky.

I pretended I didn't hear him. When I had finished my picture, I put my pink glasses back on.

Soon art class was over. Ms. Colman gave us two worksheets full of subtraction problems. I switched from my pink to my blue glasses.

"Four-eyes!" said Ricky.

I was getting a little bit mad. But Hannie nudged me. She passed me a note which I opened up in my lap. With my glasses on, I could read it perfectly. It said: *Yicky Ricky is picky and sticky.*

I tried not to giggle.

Then I worked very hard on my subtraction problems. And guess what — after

lunch, Ms. Colman gave our worksheets back. I got 100 percent on both of them. Two 100 percents!

"I'm very proud of you, Karen," said Ms. Colman.

In reading class, I followed all the directions on the board and I did all of my work perfectly. I had to switch my glasses a lot, so Ricky called me Four-eyes and Bat-woman about five times. But what did I care? I got 100 percents on everything!

At the end of the day, Ms. Colman called me to her desk. It was Free Reading time, and I was just starting a book about a bear named Paddington. I hated to put it down.

But I hated even more to hear what Ms. Colman said: "Karen, I am going to move you to the front row of the classroom."

"But why?" I cried. Had she seen Hannie pass me the note? Hannie and Nancy and I had tried so hard to be good. "I've been good." I told her. "At least, I have *tried* to be good."

That was the honest truth.

"Karen, this doesn't have anything to do with being good or bad," Ms. Colman told me. "It's because of your eyes. You'll see better up front. I've noticed how many times you had to switch your glasses today."

I nodded. That *had* been a pain.

"So please take your things out of your desk. You will be trading desks with Hank Reubens. He can move to your old seat. I'll talk to him while you clear out your desk."

I thought of saying that I did not want to

trade with Hank Reubens, but you don't argue with teachers. Even one as nice as Ms. Colman.

Of course everyone wanted to know what Hank and I were doing when they saw us taking the things out of our desks. Finally Ms. Colman said, "Karen is moving to the front row, boys and girls. She will be able to see the board better from there."

When Hank and I had traded places, I was sitting right in front of Ms. Colman's desk. I liked that. But I did not like leaving Hannie and Nancy behind. And I bet they did not like sitting next to Hank. Hank bites the erasers off of his pencils.

As if these things were not bad enough, Ricky thought of a new nickname for me. When school was over that day, he walked by me singing, *"Teacher's pet, teacher's pet. Karen is the teacher's pet."*

I will get you, Ricky Torres, I thought.

I put on my pink glasses and left the classroom.

Baby Karen

I thought about Ricky Torres all weekend. How could I get back at him? He had called me Four-eyes and Bat-woman and the teacher's pet. I already called him Yicky Ricky. And I had called him Mr. Smarty-pants. But those things did not seem bad enough. Besides, it was not at all nice of him to tease me just because I had to get glasses. Nobody teased him when he got a cast on his ankle.

On Sunday afternoon, Nancy came over. She found me in my room, sitting in my rocking chair. Goosie was in my lap. I was wearing my pink glasses. Goosie was wearing the blue ones.

"What are you doing?" asked Nancy.

"Goosie and I are thinking of ways to get back at Yicky Ricky. He is so mean."

"And picky and sticky," added Nancy. (She had seen Hannie's note.)

Nancy and I laughed.

"What ideas have you thought of?" asked Nancy.

"None," I answered. "Not one single good one."

The next morning I could think of just one thing to do about Ricky and my glasses. I forgot to bring my glasses to school. Actually, I forgot them on purpose. I left both pairs of glasses on the bureau in my bedroom. Mrs. Dawes was driving Nancy and me to school, so Mommy did not see me run out of our house without my glasses.

I smiled all the way to school. If I didn't wear my glasses, then Ricky couldn't tease me, could he? He would look pretty silly calling me Four-eyes or Bat-woman when I didn't even have glasses on.

But the first thing Ms. Colman said when I walked into our classroom with Nancy was, "Karen, where are your glasses?"

"Huh?" I replied, as if I had just realized I wasn't wearing them.

"Are they in your book bag?" asked Ms. Colman. "You'd better put the pink ones on right now. You know you're supposed to wear them all the time."

I pretended to look through my book bag. "I — I guess I left them at home," I told Ms. Colman.

"Both pairs?"

I nodded.

"Karen," she said firmly, "you must remember them from now on."

"Okay," I replied. "Tomorrow I will wear them for sure."

I thought that was the end of that. Ricky came in and couldn't find anything to tease me about. I felt very happy. Until someone knocked on the door to our classroom during subtraction time.

In walked . . . Mommy! She called me over to the doorway.

"Ms. Colman phoned," she whispered. (I just knew everyone was watching Mommy and me. I was gigundo embarrassed.) "She said you forgot your glasses today. So here you go." She handed me both pairs. "And from now on, no more forgetting. You *must*

wear your glasses all the time. It's very important."

Mommy was forgetting to whisper. I know everyone heard her.

So I whispered, "Okay," and, "Thank you."

Then Mommy left.

In the cafeteria that day, Ricky came to the table Hannie and Nancy and I were sitting at.

"Ha-ha, Bat-woman," he said to me. "Now you *have* to wear your glasses when we have our pictures taken. Your mother said you must wear them all the time. If you don't, she'll be really upset . . . Baby Karen."

Oh, no. What a problem. Ricky was right. I *would* have to wear my glasses. And he had a new name for me. Baby Karen.

What was I going to do?

Mean Things to Do to Ricky Torres

I was so mad that when I got home after school that day I went right to my room. I put on my blue glasses. I sat at my desk with a piece of paper in front of me. Across the top of it I wrote:

Mean Things to Do to Ricky Torres

Then I thought for awhile. Finally I wrote:

1. Tell him he smells.

That wasn't true, but so what. I was not as blind as a bat, either.

Then I wrote:

2. Put my strawberry eraser in his desk and tell Ms. Colman he stole it.

That was really mean, plus it would be lying. I would never do it. But I left it on the list anyway.

Next I wrote:

3. Tattle on him to Ms. Colman about the names he calls me.

61

4. Put a worm in his lunch box.
5. Put pepper (lots of it) in his lunch box.

I paused to think. I decided I needed ten mean things. So I added:

6. Hide his reading book.
7. Tell him his eyes have turned orange. Then have Nancy tell him his eyes have turned orange. Then have Hannie and maybe Natalie tell him his eyes have turned orange. Laugh at him if he checks them in a mirror.
8. Tell him that Mollie Foley from Mrs. Fulton's room says she's in love with him and wants to kiss him on the playground.
9. Ask him to see-saw with me during recess. When my end is on the ground, I'll roll off and say, "Ooh, my leg," like I'm hurt. He will crash to the ground.
10. Tell him he's adopted.

I told Andrew he was adopted right after Daddy and Elizabeth adopted Emily. Andrew was very upset.

* * *

The next day, I folded my list up eight times. I put it in my lunch box. I brought it to school. I felt very smug, even with my glasses on.

I was all set to get back at Ricky Torres. But Ricky was absent.

Ricky's Glasses

Okay. So Ricky had a cold or something. I was sure he would be in school the next day. Since I was so sure, I brought the list with me again.

I was right. Ricky *was* in school. And — and he was wearing . . . *glasses!*

At first I thought he was making fun of me. His glasses were pretty ugly. They were brown and squarish.

"Very funny, Ricky," I said, as he slumped down at his desk. "Okay, you can take them off now." I was about to add, "By the way, did you know that you're adopted?''

But Ricky looked like he was trying not to cry. So I closed my mouth. When I opened it again, all I said was, "What's wrong?"

"They're real," Ricky whispered. "The glasses. They're real. I had to get them, just like you. That's where I was yesterday. At the eye doctor's and everything. Only I just have one pair of glasses."

I hardly knew what to say. Ricky had called me Four-eyes and Bat-woman. I could call him a name now. If I wanted. Only I could see how bad he felt.

Plus a big group of kids was gathering around Ricky. Ricky looked like he wished he were anywhere but sitting at his desk, wearing glasses.

"Four-eyes!" said Hank Reubens.

"Bat-*man!*" cried Nancy gleefully.

"Square-eyes!" added Hannie.

My friends were getting back at Ricky for me. Fine. He could stay in the back of the room with his glasses, and I could stay in the front with my glasses, and we would not have to bother each other at all.

That was what I thought. But guess what Ms. Colman did as soon as she had taken attendance that morning.

She smiled at our class. Then she said, "Boys and girls, we have another new glasses-wearer, so we will have to switch some places again. Ricky, you need to sit up front with Karen and Natalie."

Ricky groaned.

I could have told him there was no point. A few minutes later, he was sitting *right next to me*. Jannie Gilbert had moved back to Ricky's old seat.

Ricky and I looked at each other. Ricky narrowed his eyes. Then he stuck his tongue out at me — just the tip, so that Ms. Colman wouldn't see.

I stuck the tip of my tongue out at him. Then I passed him a note. It read: LEAVE ME ALONE!

Ricky passed one back. His read: REMER-BER SKOOL PICSHERS. (Ricky is not a very good speller.)

I took Ricky's note, corrected it, gave him a D+, and passed it back to him.

Ricky stuck the tip of his tongue out at me again.

I did not pay one speck of attention.

Later, Ms. Colman handed back some spelling tests. I got another 100 percent. Ricky got a 55 percent. He had spelled almost half of the words wrong. So he threw a spitball at me. It was disgusting. I knocked

it on the floor. It rolled under Ms. Colman's desk, but she did not see it.

I raised my hand. "Ms. Colman?"

"Yes, Karen?"

"Ricky threw a spitball at me. It's under your desk."

Ricky looked like he wanted to kill me.

"One more spitball, Ricky," said Ms. Colman, "and you will miss recess."

Ricky waited until Ms. Colman was helping someone in the back of the room. Then he opened his mouth. I think he was going to call me a name. But he closed his mouth instead. No matter what name he called me, I could call him one back.

I made a decision. No matter how mad I was at Ricky, I would not make him feel worse about his glasses.

Just before lunch, I threw away my list of mean things to do to Ricky.

Ricky Is a Gir-irl!

During recess on most days, Hannie and Nancy and I play hopscotch. We are very good. Sometimes we can get all the way to the fourth square on one turn. And we never miss on the hopping part, only the stone-throwing part.

On the day Ricky first wore his glasses to school, we were having an especially good game. It was my turn. My playing had gotten a lot better since I started wearing glasses. I was about to throw to the fifth square when I heard:

"Aughh! Cut it out!"

It was Ricky, and he had made me miss.

I whirled around. "What did you have to scream like that for?" I shouted to him. "You made me — "

I stopped. I looked at Hannie and Nancy. They looked at me.

Ricky was in trouble.

The other boys in our class had crowded around him.

"Four-eyes!" cried Hank Reubens.

"Bat-man!" called someone else.

Then Bobby Gianelli, who is a big bully, made a grab for Ricky's glasses. He tried to snatch them right off his face. "Cut it *out!*" yelled Ricky again. He darted away from Bobby.

"Hey!" hooted Hank. "Guess what. Ricky is a gir-irl! Karen wears glasses, Natalie wears glasses, Ms. Colman wears glasses. Now Ricky's got 'em!"

"Yeah, he *is* a girl!" cried Bobby.

Bobby grabbed for Ricky's glasses again. That time, he almost got them.

70

I couldn't stand it any longer. I raced over to the boys.

"You stop that!" I yelled. "You leave Ricky alone! Don't touch his glasses, Bobby. Glasses are very, very expensive."

"*Yeah*," said Hannie and Nancy firmly. They were standing beside me.

Ricky looked miserable. I knew just how he felt. Or anyway, I knew almost how he felt. I sure was glad that nobody had made a ring around me on the playground and tried to take off my glasses.

"And Ricky is not a girl just because he wears glasses," I added.

Everyone had stopped yelling. They were staring at me. "My daddy wears glasses," I said, "and my stepdaddy wears glasses. . . . *So there.*"

Ricky was just staring at me. I couldn't tell what he was thinking.

Bobby backed away from Ricky. He looked sort of ashamed.

But Ricky yelled, "Shut up, Karen! Just shut up! I don't need help from a *girl*. Go

back to your dumb old hopscotch game."
Then he pushed his way through the circle
of kids. "I can stand up for myself, Karen!"
he cried. And he added, "Ugly-puss." He
ran away to the swings and sat by himself.

I stood where I was. I felt like I had been
stung.

A couple of the boys snickered at me, but
Hannie said, "Come on, Karen. Let's go
back to our game."

"Yeah," added Nancy. "You can take
your turn over. Ricky made you miss before.
That wasn't fair."

But all I could say was, "Ricky has a new
name for me. Ugly-puss."

"Call him Ugly-puss back," suggested
Hannie.

"No," I replied. "What's the point?"

Hannie and Nancy and I finished our
game. Nancy won.

"Are you having trouble seeing?" Nancy
asked me.

I shook my head. I could not say anything.

But it didn't matter. The bell rang. Recess was over.

Ricky and I did not speak to each other all afternoon. We did not stick the tips of our tongues out at each other. We did not even look at each other. I guess we were too embarrassed.

I could not wait to get home.

Ugly-puss

As soon as I got home that afternoon, I ran upstairs to my room. I did not stop for a snack. I did not stop even when Andrew said, "Hey, Karen, Mommy bought peanuts today."

I love peanuts, but peanuts would not make me feel better.

"No, thank you," I said to Andrew.

I closed the door to my room.

"Ugly-puss," I said out loud. Was I really ugly when I wore my glasses?

Then I thought a horrible thought. What

if I was ugly with*out* my glasses? What if I was just plain ugly? Maybe I was silly to think I could be a movie star.

Knock, knock, knock.

Someone was at my door.

"Go away, Andrew," I said. I still didn't want any peanuts.

But somebody who wasn't Andrew said, "It's not Andrew. It's me."

Nancy.

I did not really want to see Nancy, either. But I said, "Come in."

Nancy opened the door. Then she closed it behind her.

"Am I *really* ugly?" I asked Nancy.

"You? Ugly? Of course not."

"But Ricky called me an Ugly-puss."

"He was just mad because he has to wear glasses now, too."

I didn't say anything.

"Karen, you hardly look any different when you wear your glasses," said Nancy.

"I don't? Watch this." I was wearing my pink glasses. I put the blue ones on Goosie.

"There," I said. "See how different Goosie looks?"

"Goosie," said Nancy, "is a stuffed cat. No one expects cats to wear glasses. That's why he looks different."

"But maybe I really am ugly," I said to Nancy. "Even without glasses."

"Just because Ricky said so?" replied Nancy. "Do you believe everything Ricky says? If he told you you were a cow, would you believe him?"

I giggled. "No."

"Okay. Then forget what he said. I am your friend. And I am saying you look just fine, with your glasses on or with your glasses off."

"Like a movie star?" I asked.

Nancy shrugged. "I don't know. Some people in the movies wear glasses, some don't."

"That's true," I admitted. I felt better. "Want some peanuts, Nancy?"

"Sure," she replied, and we ran downstairs to find Andrew.

The next day, I did not want to wear my glasses in school. But I wore them anyway.

I did not want to sit next to Ricky, but I sat next to him anyway.

I didn't look at him. I didn't talk to him. I just did my work. And I got 100 percents everywhere. Switching my glasses helped a lot.

That day, Ricky called me a name every time I switched my glasses. That was seven times — five times in the morning, and two times in the afternoon.

On Friday, he didn't bother.

I felt like I wasn't even sitting next to him.

I had almost forgotten about glasses and movie-star smiles and Ricky. Then Ms. Colman said, "Boys and girls, remember that we will have our pictures taken on Monday. So get ready to look your best, and practice your smiles."

Oh, no. School pictures. Somehow, I had almost forgotten about them, too.

Next to me, Ricky began to snicker.

Ms. Colman heard him. "Mr. Torres?" she said. "Is there something funny that you'd like to share with the class?"

"No," answered Ricky. I peeked over at him just long enough to see that his face had turned red.

Good.

But what was I going to do about Monday? I would have to think very hard over the weekend.

Karen's Problem

That Friday wasn't just any Friday. It was a special Friday. It was a Going-to-Daddy's Friday.

I was excited and nervous. I was excited because Andrew and I are always excited about going to Daddy's. I was nervous because no one at the big house had seen me in my glasses yet. Not even David Michael. (He doesn't go to my school.)

Would David Michael tease me? He might, since sometimes he can be just like Ricky. Sam is a big tease, too. So I was nervous.

When Mommy let Andrew and me out of the car at Daddy's, she called, "Good-bye, Karen! Good-bye, Andrew! Have fun!"

"Good-bye, Mommy! We will!" we called back.

But I did not run to Daddy's front door as fast as usual.

Andrew did, though. He opened it and stepped inside.

I followed him. I did not call out, "We're here!" like I usually do.

So Andrew did it. "We're here," he said.

Even though his voice is not as loud as mine, everyone came running.

"Oh, Karen. Your glasses!" exclaimed Daddy. "I like them very much."

"You chose the perfect frames," said Elizabeth.

"I did?" I began to smile.

"You look distinguished," added Sam.

"Really?" I didn't know what "distinguished" meant and I was afraid to ask. Sometimes Sam teases me with big words.

But Charlie helped me out. He said, "Sam

means you look dignified and important. Like a professor or something. A *pretty* professor," Charlie added quickly. (Charlie doesn't like to hurt people's feelings.)

"Kristy?" I asked.

"You look like my Karen," she said.

That was just what I needed to hear.

The rest of the evening was fine, except for one little thing. When my big-house family sat down to dinner, David Michael began calling me Professor. I do not think he was being mean. I think he was trying to be nice. He had heard Charlie say I look like a professor. And he knows that Charlie is usually nice and doesn't tease.

But I did not want to look like a professor. I wanted to look like a movie star.

I decided to talk to Kristy.

Bedtime is usually a good talking time, so after we had finished our reading, I said, "Kristy?"

"Yes?" Kristy was plugging in the night-light that I got at Disney World.

"Monday is school-picture day," I told her.

"Oh, great! Do you know what you're going to wear?"

"Yes. I know about everything except my glasses. I can't decide whether to wear them. Ricky Torres says I'm an Ugly-puss."

"You are not an Ugly-puss," said Kristy. She sat down on the bed and put her arm around me.

"I think I look like a dork with my glasses on."

"Then don't wear them."

"Mommy gets mad when I don't wear them," I replied.

"She won't mind for just a minute."

"She might. Besides, Mommy never takes off her glasses when she has her picture taken. Neither does Natalie. Neither does Ms. Colman. I think," I said finally, "that I will feel like a dork if I leave them on, and I will feel like a wimp if I take them off. I do not know *what* to do."

Kristy gave me a butterfly kiss on my cheek. "I have an idea," she said. "I'll tell you about it tomorrow. Try to go to sleep now, okay?"

"Okay," I said. "Thank you, Kristy."

"You're welcome."

I fell asleep right away.

Spectacles

"Today," Kristy told me at breakfast on Saturday, "we are going to the library, Karen."

"And I will drive you there," Charlie added grandly.

"Why are we going to the library?" I asked. I like the library a lot, but Kristy and Charlie sounded quite mysterious.

"You'll see," was all Kristy would answer.

"Hey, Professor," said David Michael from across the table. "Will you return my library books for me?"

"Sure," I replied. I still could not decide whether I liked being called Professor.

Charlie dropped Kristy and me off at the library just as it was opening. Kristy led me into the children's room. We were the only people there, except for a librarian.

"May I help you?" she asked us.

"Thank you," said Kristy, "but we have to do this ourselves. I want to show my sister some pictures of people who wear glasses."

The librarian smiled. I frowned. What was Kristy up to?

Kristy took me by the hand. She walked me to a shelf labeled HOLIDAY BOOKS. She pulled out a bunch of Christmas stories.

"Notice anything?" she asked as we leafed through the books.

"Santa Claus wears glasses!" I exclaimed. "So does Mrs. Claus sometimes."

Then Kristy went to another shelf. She handed me a copy of *Winnie-the-Pooh*. I love that book.

"Take a look through it," said Kristy.

"Owl wears glasses!" I cried. Then I remembered that I was in a library and should keep my voice down.

Next, Kristy handed me a huge, fat book of stories with pictures by a man named Walt Disney. "Look!" I whispered loudly. "Geppetto wears glasses in *Pinocchio*, and the White Rabbit wears them in *Alice in Wonderland*, and John in *Peter Pan*, and even Scrooge McDuck. And Doc! He's my favorite

dwarf. Kristy, let's see if Jacob Two-Two wears glasses."

We checked, but he doesn't. I was disappointed — until Kristy helped me find a book called *Spectacles* about a pair of *magic* glasses.

"Boy," I said as we left the library with *Spectacles* under my arm. "An awful lot of important people wear glasses — even if most of them *are* boys!"

School-Picture Day

On Monday morning, I woke up in my bed at the little house. It was school-picture day. I still did not know whether I was going to wear my glasses. I *liked* my glasses okay. I just did not know whether to wear them.

"Karen?" said Mommy. She stuck her head in my door. "Are you awake?"

"Mmm," I replied. I was mostly awake.

"Don't forget what day this is."

"I already remembered."

Mommy laughed. "Do you want some

help choosing your clothes, or do you know what you're going to wear?"

"I think I will wear my dress that is blue on top and blue and black plaid on the bottom. I will wear a blue ribbon in my hair."

"Perfect," said Mommy. "That is a very good choice."

Mommy drove Nancy and me to school that morning. Nancy was ready for her

picture, too. She was wearing a red sweater over a white blouse. On the collar of the blouse were red flowers with green leaves. And tied on one side of her head was a huge red bow.

We were very excited.

The ride to school seemed to take forever. When Mommy finally pulled up in front of Stoneybrook Academy, she turned to look at me.

"Karen?" she asked. "Are you going to wear your glasses when the photographer takes your picture?"

I sighed. "I don't know, Mommy," I answered. "I really don't know."

"That's okay, sweetie," she said.

But she didn't say whether to wear them or not. I knew I would have to decide for myself. At least Mommy would not be mad if I took the glasses off for my picture. That just showed how much Ricky knew.

Nyah, nyah, nyah.

Now all I had to do was decide whether to be a dork or a wimp.

Nancy and I walked to our classroom. Every kid who came in looked very dressed up. Some of the boys were even wearing suits and ties.

I checked the glasses-wearers. Natalie's were on. So were Ricky's. But he might take them off later. My pink ones were on, of course.

When Ms. Colman came into the room, she clapped her hands.

"Please take your seats, boys and girls," she said.

We sat down. We stopped talking.

"The cameraman is here," announced Ms. Colman. "He is setting up his equipment in the gym. The kindergarteners and first-graders will have their pictures taken soon. Then it will be our turn. You will have your individual pictures taken first. Afterward, we will have our class picture taken."

Well, the little kids sure took their time. Our class waited and waited for them. What could possibly take so long?

But at last the school secretary called Ms. Colman on the intercom.

"Your class may go to the gym now," she said.

"Thank you," Ms. Colman replied. "Okay, class. Line up at the door — quietly."

We lined up, but I don't know how quiet we were. It's hard to be quiet when you are very, very excited.

I wiggled in between Hannie and Nancy. I noticed that Ricky was at the head of the line.

He is so pushy.

Our line filed out of our classroom and headed for the gym.

"Here we go!" I said to Hannie and Nancy.

CLICK!

When we reached the gym, the first-graders were still there. They were not finished yet. Boo.

"The secretary called us too early," I told Hannie and Nancy. "Now we will have to wait in line."

I do not like waiting in line.

But at last the first-graders left. The photographer turned to our class.

"Is everybody ready?" he asked.

"Yes!" we cried.

"Who's first?"

"Me! I'm first!" said Ricky. He was still at the head of the line.

The photographer led Ricky to a chair in front of a pale blue screen. He stood behind his big camera. "Smile!" he said to Ricky.

"Okay," Ricky replied. But before he smiled, he took off his glasses. He looked at me and stuck out his tongue. *Then* he looked at the photographer and smiled.

"What a wimp," I whispered to Hannie and Nancy. But I wasn't sure I meant it. If I took my glasses off, too, then I could give my best movie-star smile.

CLICK! The photographer took Ricky's picture.

Natalie was next. She sat in front of the blue screen.

"Smile!" said the photographer.

Natalie smiled. She was wearing her glasses.

I looked at Ms. Colman. I imagined her standing with our class when we had the group picture taken. Her glasses would be on. And suddenly I knew what I was going to do. Only I had to get something out of my desk in our classroom first.

"Save my place!" I whispered loudly to Hannie.

"Where are you going?" she asked me.

"Can't tell. It's a secret."

I ran to Ms. Colman. I whispered my secret in her ear. Ms. Colman smiled. Then she gave me permission to go to our classroom. When I reached it, I took something out of my desk and ran back to the gym.

I got there just in time. Hannie was having her picture taken. My turn would come next.

When the photographer called to me, I walked proudly to the chair in front of the screen. I left my pink glasses on. Then I pulled the something out of the pocket of my dress — my blue glasses. They were fastened to a chain that the optometrist had given me. I had not used the chain before, but I needed it now. I slipped the chain over my head so that I was wearing the blue glasses like a necklace.

Now it was my turn to stick my tongue out at Ricky. Then I smiled at the photographer and his camera went CLICK! I had worn *both* pairs of glasses in *my* picture.

Ricky stared at me with his mouth open.

When all of my classmates had had their pictures taken, the photographer led us to some risers against the wall of the gym.

"Okay," he said, "taller kids in back, shorter kids in front."

When we were finally organized I was standing between Nancy and Yicky Ricky. Hannie was next to Nancy. Everyone was smiling.

And Ricky was wearing his glasses.

That afternoon on the playground I saw Ricky sitting on a swing by himself. I left Hannie and Nancy and ran over to him.

"Hey, Ricky," I said.

"Hey," he answered.

"Did you know," I began, "that Geppetto and the White Rabbit and Santa Claus all wear glasses?"

"Really?" replied Ricky. He sounded interested. So I told him about Owl and Doc and John and Scrooge McDuck, too.

When I was finished, Ricky said, "I'm sorry I called you names."

I decided that maybe Yicky Ricky wasn't yicky after all.

Love, Karen

One week and four days later was a very special day. It was a Going-to-Daddy's Friday. It was also the day we got our school pictures back.

That was so much fun! I just love opening the envelope and seeing the pictures inside. There are two big, big ones. There are four medium-sized ones. There are sixteen tiny ones. The tiny ones are in rows on a sheet, and you have to cut them apart. And then there is the class picture, with everyone together.

I looked happily at the class picture. There I was, wearing both pairs of glasses. There was Ricky with his glasses and Ms. Colman with her glasses and Natalie with *her* glasses. It was the most wonderful picture I had ever seen.

"What do you think?" I asked Hannie and Nancy. They were examining their pictures, too.

"Great!" said Hannie.

"Neat!" said Nancy.

I think Mommy was surprised when she looked at the pictures and saw that I was wearing two pairs of glasses. But then she said, "I am proud of you, Karen." So I still felt happy.

Mommy kept one big picture and two medium pictures for her and Seth. The other big picture and medium pictures were for Daddy and Elizabeth. All the little ones were for me. So was the class picture.

When Andrew and I got to Daddy's that night, I was so, so, so excited.

"Here are my pictures! Here are my pictures!'' I cried, before I had even taken my jacket off.

"Pretty nice, Professor," said David Michael.

"Beautiful, " said Daddy and Elizabeth.

"They look just like my Karen," said Kristy.

After dinner, I took the little pictures up to my bedroom. I found a pair of scissors and sat down at my table. Then I put on

my blue glasses. Very carefully, I cut the pictures apart.

"There," I said to Moosie. "Now I have to sign them."

I wrote "Love, Karen" on the back of every picture.

Here are the people the pictures were for: Mommy, Daddy, Seth, Elizabeth (for their wallets), Nannie, Kristy, Charlie, Sam, David Michael, Andrew, Emily, Hannie, Nancy, Natalie, my friend Amanda Delaney, and Ricky Torres.

I knew just how I would give people my pictures, too. I would hold each one out and say, "Here. This is for you from me."

Except for Ricky's picture. I would hide Ricky's picture in his desk and let him find it by himself.

I sighed. That was a good idea. Then I took off my blue glasses. I put on the pink ones. I ran downstairs. It was time to start handing out my school pictures.

About the Author

ANN M. MARTIN lives in New York City and loves animals. Her cat, Mouse, knows how to take the phone off the hook.

Other books by Ann M. Martin that you might enjoy are *Stage Fright*, *Me and Katie (the Pest)*, and the books in *The Baby-sitters Club* series.

Ann likes ice cream, the beach, and *I Love Lucy*. And she has her own little sister, whose name is Jane.

ENTER THE

B·A·B·Y·S·I·T·T·E·R·S

Little Sister ™

G·I·V·E·A·W·A·Y·!

WIN A CAMERA!

Smile!. You can win a Vivitar Compact 35MM camera! It has a built-in flash and fits right in your pocket (5 1/4" x 3"). Bring it to school! Take pictures of your friends! Karen loved her school picture — you won't have to wait for yours! Enter the Baby-sitters Little Sister Giveaway. Just fill in the coupon below and return by November 30, 1989.

Rules: Entries must be postmarked by November 30, 1989. Winners will be picked at random and notified by mail. No purchase necessary. Valid only in the U.S.A. Void where prohibited. Taxes on prizes are the responsibility of the winners and their families. Employees of Scholastic Inc., its agencies, affiliates, subsidiaries, and their immediate families not eligible. For a complete list of winners, send a stamped, self-addressed envelope to The Baby-sitters Little Sister Giveaway, Contest Winners List, at the address provided below.

Fill in the coupon below or write the information on a 3" x 5" piece of paper and mail to:
THE BABY-SITTERS LITTLE SISTER GIVEAWAY,
Scholastic Inc., P.O. Box 665, Cooper Station, New York, NY 10276.

Baby-sitters Little Sister Giveaway

Where did you buy this Baby-sitters Little Sister book?
❑ Bookstore ❑ Drug Store ❑ Supermarket
❑ Discount Store ❑ Book Club ❑ Book Fair

Other _____ (specify)

25 Winners!

Name _____ Age _____

Street _____

City _____ State _____ Zip _____

BLS389